# My Dad's Secret

PRAISE FOR *STORYSHARES*

"One of the brightest innovators and game-changers in the education industry."
– Forbes

"Your success in applying research-validated practices to promote literacy serves as a valuable model for other organizations seeking to create evidence-based literacy programs."

- Library of Congress

"We need powerful social and educational innovation, and Storyshares is breaking new ground. The organization addresses critical problems facing our students and teachers. I am excited about the strategies it brings to the collective work of making sure every student has an equal chance in life."
– Teach For America

"Around the world, this is one of the up-and-coming trailblazers changing the landscape of literacy and education."
- International Literacy Association

"It's the perfect idea. There's really nothing like this. I mean wow, this will be a wonderful experience for young people."    - Andrea Davis Pinkney, Executive Director, Scholastic

"Reading for meaning opens opportunities for a lifetime of learning. Providing emerging readers with engaging texts that are designed to offer both challenges and support for each individual will improve their lives for years to come. Storyshares is a wonderful start."
- David Rose, Co-founder of CAST & UDL

# My Dad's Secret

## Mary Francis

STORYSHARES

Story Share, Inc.
New York. Boston. Philadelphia

Published in the United States by Story Share, Inc.

Storyshares
Story Share, Inc.
24 N. Bryn Mawr Avenue #340
Bryn Mawr, PA 19010-3304
www.storyshares.org

*Inspiring reading with a new kind of book.*

**Interest Level:** Middle School
**Grade Level Equivalent:** 3.0

9798885979108

Book design by Storyshares

Printed in the United States of America

Storyshares Presents

# 1

"Abby, are you even listening?"

Abby shuffled the paper she had been doodling on and looked up. "Yes, Mrs. Sherman. I was just deciding what I would write about."

Mrs. Sherman sighed and went back to whatever she'd been talking about.

The truth was, Abby had stopped listening a while ago. She hated the whole idea of the new assignment.

This creative writing class was not nearly as exciting as she had hoped when she'd signed up. Well, that wasn't exactly true. It was probably exciting if you had exciting things to write about.

Abby did not.

"All right, since you all understand the assignment, I'll let you get started." Mrs. Sherman went back to her desk and sat down. "This should be a fun project for everyone!"

Abby snorted. The assignment was to write about your family history. Abby looked around the classroom. She could see that her classmates were excited.

The room was buzzing as everyone shared stories with each other. As she listened to them talk, she grew jealous of their family histories.

Roberto's dad was from South America. Roberto was talking about his family's journey to the United States. It took them two years to get to the United States. Roberto had so many stories to share about what they went through.

Diya was talking about her family's traditions. Her family celebrated Diwali, a holiday Abby had never heard of. It sounded like a lot of fun. They celebrated it over five days. Each day had its own traditions. It was a festival of lights. The holiday was celebrated with a lot of candles. They had all kinds of sweets and treats and tables full of different foods. There was even a day with fireworks. Kind of like Christmas, Thanksgiving, and Fourth of July—all at the same time!

Jamal was eager to start writing about his grandfather, who was a war hero. He had been injured during the war. Even though his grandfather was hurt, he still saved the lives of two other people. He received medals when he got home.

Nellie's family came to America on a boat. They came through Ellis Island in New York. Everyone had just learned about Ellis Island and how it was a major immigration center in the old days. The kids gathered around Nellie when she started telling her story.

Abby had no interesting stories to share. How could she make a boring story into something fun? Worse, the assignment wasn't going to just be turned in to the teacher. The class had been told they would be reading their papers in front of everyone.

Abby knew her classmates were going to be so bored when she read her paper.

# 2

That afternoon, Abby walked home thinking about her assignment.

Her mom's parents were from California. They had been in the United States for a long time. Before that, her family was from England. There was nothing interesting about how they came to the United States.

Her great-great-grandmother came over with her whole family when she was nineteen. She met Abby's great-great-grandfather when she first got to the country.

He had been talking to the new passengers and writing down their names when they arrived. They liked each other.

He got her family a place to stay. Soon, the two of them started dating.

The next year, they got married. That was it. Pretty basic compared to the other kids in class.

While she knew about her mom's parents, she didn't know anything about her dad's.

The more Abby thought about it, the stranger that seemed.

*Had they died? Did they die when her dad was young?* Maybe he didn't know much about them.

*But, if that were true, who raised him? Why didn't her parents ever talk about them?*

All kinds of thoughts went through Abby's head. She started making up reasons why no one ever talked about her dad's parents.

*Were they abusive? Did her dad have a bad childhood?* That would be so sad.

Abby wondered if her dad had been raised in foster care by many families.

# 3

At dinner, Abby's mom asked why she was so quiet. She shrugged and continued eating.

"Everything OK at school?"

Abby stopped eating and looked at her dad. "Dad, where are your parents from? How come we never talk about them?"

Abby's dad quickly looked up from his plate. "What? What brought that up?"

"I have an assignment at school. We have to tell a story about our family's ancestry... where we come from," said Abby.

Abby's mom and dad exchanged glances.

Abby's mom answered in a way that seemed too happy. "Well, did you know that your great-great-grandmother came over to America from England? She met your great-great-grandfather as she was filling out her paperwork!"

"Yes, Mom, I know." Abby looked back at her dad. "Where are your parents from? I don't know anything about them. I don't know anything about your side of the family at all."

Abby's dad was now focused on his plate. "Well— they live across the country in Virginia."

"They're alive?!" Abby exclaimed. "Why don't we ever talk to them? My friends have grandparents that live all over the place. They always talk to them. Why don't we?"

Abby's dad didn't say anything. He just kept eating.

"Not everyone gets along with their parents, Abby," said Abby's mom. "Enough of this. Let's get dinner cleaned up. Then I'll see what I can find for you about your great-great-grandmother's trip from England!"

Abby's mom got up and started clearing the table. Her dad got up and headed to his office.

# 4

Abby was frustrated. She wanted to know more. She went to her room and started looking for information on the internet.

Searching for her dad's name didn't get her much. Not anything about his parents, anyway.

She wanted to search her grandparents' names— but she didn't even know what they were.

Searching for just their last name got too many results.

Abby started exploring family history sites.  She found various things about her mom's family. Nothing about her dad.

She couldn't even find his birth certificate. There was nothing out there from his life before he got married.

Abby quickly shut her laptop when a knock sounded on her bedroom door.

Abby's mom walked in holding some papers. "I have some information about Grandma's trip to America. There's even a photo from when she first arrived! I just got off the phone with her. She said you should call her anytime. You can ask as many questions as you want."

"Thanks Mom, but I really want to know more about dad's family. Do you know why he doesn't talk to them? Did he have a bad childhood?"

"Oh Abby," her mother said. "That's all in the past. Dad didn't have a bad childhood. He just doesn't like thinking about the past. It upsets him. Please let this go. I'm sure Grandma will have some fun stories to share with you. Call her tomorrow!"

Abby's mom put the papers down and left the room.

My Dad's Secret

# 5

The next day in school, all Abby thought about was her dad's family. She wanted to know more.

One of her classmates was worried because she was adopted. She didn't know a lot about her family either. But her parents were helping her to learn more. *And anyway, being adopted was interesting too!*

Abby decided she would call her Gram after school. Maybe she would know something about her dad's parents.

The rest of the day, Abby kept staring at the clock. She wished the day would end. When it did, she could get home and call her Gram.

The bell finally rang at the end of the day. Abby ran out of school. She ran home. She didn't stop to talk to her mom. Instead, she rushed upstairs to her room and called her Gram.

After telling her Gram about her day, Abby asked if she knew anything about her dad's family. There was a long pause. Her Gram said she didn't know much.

She said their names were Stuart and Patty. Abby hung up the phone. She was so excited!

Maybe this extra information would be enough to find out more about them!

# 6

That night, Abby asked her dad what part of Virginia his parents lived in. Her dad sighed. He said they moved a lot, so he wasn't sure.

"Well—where did they live last time you knew?" Abby asked.

Abby's father was clearly getting upset.

"Abby—please stop asking," he said. "We don't agree on some things. So we don't stay in touch now."

"What kind of things?" Abby asked.

"All kinds of things," her dad answered. "They aren't bad people. They just have different views than I do."

"But like what? Do they know about me? Do they know you had me?"

"I don't really know, Abby. Some things are just better left alone. Can you stop asking about this?" Abby's dad got up from the table and went to his office.

"Why is he so mad?" Abby asked her mom

"He's not really mad. He just doesn't like to talk about them. He might even be sad," her mom said. "Abby, I told you—you need to let this go. Stop asking about them."

Lying in bed later, Abby knew she could not let it go. The less she was able to find, the more she wanted to know.

# 7

Abby woke up Saturday morning and heard her parents getting ready to go to her cousin's party.

She went into the kitchen and sat at the table. "I don't feel good. I have a headache and I'm really tired. I don't think I can go today."

Her mom came over and felt her forehead.

"Thankfully, you don't seem to have a fever. We're not leaving for another hour and a half. Why don't you go rest. Maybe that will help. We'll decide a bit later. I know you really wanted to see Jill today," her mom said. "It would be a shame if you missed the party."

Abby really did want to go see her cousin. But she would not have many opportunities to stay home and make calls with no one around.

An hour later, she told her parents she still had a headache, and she wanted to stay home.

As soon as she was alone, Abby got on the computer to make a list of all her potential grandparents.

She crossed some people off the list when she did an address search. No one named Stuart or Patty was at those addresses.

But she found 23 names that might be her grandparents.

She was glad they didn't have a common last name. The search could've taken forever! Twenty-three names still seemed like a lot.

Especially because she wanted to make the phone calls before her parents came home.

# 8

No one answered the first two calls.

On the third call, she got her first answer.

"Hello?" It was a man.

"Hello!" Abby tried to sound friendly and nice. "My name is Abby Vanbruit. I'm looking for Stuart or Patty."

"Well, you're talking to Stu," he said. "But I don't know any Patty!"

"Oh. I'm sorry," Abby apologized. "I must have the wrong number."

The same things happened for several calls.

Some people didn't answer. Abby made a note to call them back later.

Some of them didn't have a name listed, just an "S." One person was named Sam. Another was named Shelia. No one was named Stuart.

"Hello?" A woman answered this time.

"Hi! My name is Abby." She hoped she still sounded friendly and nice. "I'm looking for Stuart or Patty."

"This is Patty. Can I help you?"

Abby was shocked. She was calling Stuarts—and she got Patty! This had to be it! Her stomach felt like there were butterflies in it. She could feel her heart racing.

"Hello?"

Patty's voice brought her back to the present. She wasn't even sure *what* to say. She hadn't thought this far ahead.

"Hi," she started. "My name is Abby. I, um...my dad's name is Peter Vanbruit. Do you know him? Are you his mom?"

She heard a gasp. Then the woman spoke again. "Has something happened to him? Is he all right?"

"He is fine," Abby assured her. "Yes. Yes. There's nothing wrong."

Abby paused.

"Oh. I see. What can I do for you?" the woman asked.

"I ...umm...I don't know." Abby wasn't sure what to say. She decided the truth was best. "I was just...well...I was wondering...I was working on a project for school and..."

Patty interrupted. "Does ...Peter...know you are calling me?"

"No," Abby answered honestly.

"I see. You should probably talk with him about this."

"I'm doing a project on my family history for school," Abby said quickly. "I asked him about you. He didn't really tell me much."

"How old are you, Abby?" Patty asked.

"Sixteen."

"Wow—it has been such a long time." The line was quiet for a moment before the woman spoke again. "It really is nice speaking to you, Abby. But I can't really tell you anything else. I am so sorry. I am glad you called, though. You should talk to your dad."

Abby was very disappointed. "OK. Well. Thank you. It was nice talking to you too. "

"You too, Abby. Goodbye." She sounded sad.

"Bye," Abby answered.

"Abby?" Patty spoke before she could hang up the phone.

"Yes?" Abby asked hopefully.

Patty's voice got quiet. It sounded like she was trying not to cry.

"When you talk to your dad, would you tell him his mother said hello?" Patty hung up the phone.

Abby sat there looking at the phone. *Tell her father that Patty said hello?*

*Wow.*

Abby wasn't even sure she would tell them she called. She didn't understand why they never spoke to each other.

Her dad was great. Patty—her Gram—seemed very nice too.

# My Dad's Secret

# 9

Abby was in the kitchen. She was looking in the fridge when her parents got home.

Her dad held up a stack of covered plates. "Hungry? We brought you some food—and some cake! How are you feeling?" her dad asked.

"I'm fine," she answered. "My headache is gone."

"Glad to hear it!" Her dad smiled. "We were worried about you. We left early. Jill packed up this food in case you felt better. She was disappointed you couldn't make it. She said to call her later if you feel up to it."

Abby felt guilty. Her dad was being so nice.

She had missed Jill's party, *and* she had called her grandparents after her dad told her to leave it alone.

Abby's stomach turned. Now she really did feel sick

"I called your mom today. She said to tell you she said hi," Abby blurted out.

Her dad just stared at her.

He went into the living room and sat down on the couch. He put his head in his hands.

Her mom went over and put her hand on his shoulder.

She looked at Abby. "Why? Why would you do that? You were told to leave it alone. I asked you to *please* leave it alone." Abby's mom's voice was shaking. "Did you even have a headache? Did you lie to us to stay home to do this?"

"I'm sorry." Abby was speaking quickly. "I really am. I'm really sorry. I just want to know more about where I came from. She was very nice. And...she didn't tell me anything. She said I have to talk to you, but she did say she was glad I called."

Abby turned to head to her room.

Her dad lifted his head. "She told you to say hello to me?"

"Yes. When I was hanging up. She told me she couldn't really talk to me," Abby explained. "I have to talk to you. Then she told me to tell you she said hello."

Abby was startled to see her dad's eyes filling with tears.

He sighed. He looked at her mom. "We knew this day would come. I just guess no matter how much you plan, you're never really prepared for it."

# 10

Abby's mom sat next to her dad. They motioned for Abby to come sit with them.

"Shall I, or do you want to?" Abby's mom asked her dad.

"I will," he said.

Abby was shaking as she sat and waited. She couldn't imagine what they were going to say. It had to be a big deal considering how they were acting.

"About 25 years ago," her dad started, "I fell in love with your mom. We were still in high school. We'd known each other for years. We weren't the popular kids. We had a small group of people we hung out with."

"Not popular," laughed Abby's mom. "You may as well throw it all out there, explain it completely. We weren't just '*not popular.*' We were thought of as freaks."

"Really?" asked Abby.

That didn't seem possible. Her parents were well respected. They had a lot of friends. They were very active in the community.

Abby was even more curious now. "Wow, why did they think you were freaks?"

"Well..." Her mom seemed uncomfortable. "We were different than most of the kids. We just liked different things. "

"What kind of things?" asked Abby.

Her dad thought for a moment "Just different. It's hard to explain. We were just in a smaller group of kids."

Abby wrinkled her nose as she thought. "A smaller group of kids made you feel like freaks? I don't hang out in a large group of kids, and I don't feel bad about it."

Abby's mom piped up. "There were other things. We weren't really dating much. We weren't dating the way the other kids were"

Abby shrugged. "OK. I'm not dating yet, even though a lot of kids are. It's still not weird."

"I wasn't interested in boys at the time," her mom said.

Abby's parents both looked at her. They were looking at her like they wanted her to understand something.

Abby sat there for a moment. Then she thought she understood. She looked up quickly. "You were bi? You liked boys *and* girls? Really?" she asked.

"Something like that," said Abby's dad.

Her mom spoke up. "No, I wasn't bi. I was a lesbian. I only liked girls."

"WOW!" exclaimed Abby. "That's—that's... WOW. When did you decide you liked boys?"

Her parents looked at each other. Abby's mom reached out and squeezed her dad's hand.

"The thing is," said Abby's mom, "I never did. I *am* a lesbian."

# 11

Abby just sat there looking at them. So many thoughts were running around in her head.

*Did that mean her mom and dad were just friends? How could that be?* wondered Abby.

Abby looked at the floor and shuffled her feet. She had no idea what to say.

Her dad took a deep breath. He shifted himself to the front of the couch. "Abby—I was born a girl. My name was Cassie. When I met your mom, I was a girl."

Abby gasped and stared at them. Her mind was racing as she tried to wrap her head around all of this.

"OH. MY. GOD. I feel like I am not awake right now. Is this real?" Abby asked. "You...you had a sex change?"

The room was quiet. Everyone was just sitting, looking at each other.

After a few minutes, Abby started laughing.

Her parents looked at each other. They were visibly concerned.

Her mom got up, came over, and sat beside her. "I know it is a lot to take in...a lot to hear all at once. I'm sorry. We never knew when a good time to tell you would be." Her mother sighed. "I didn't even know HOW to tell you. It is so complicated."

"No, it is fine," Abby assured her mom. "I'm laughing because I didn't think I had anything 'interesting' in my family history! But I do! This is *pretty* interesting."

Her dad spoke up. "You're going to share this with your classmates? Abby, you can't."

"Well...yes. Why wouldn't I? This IS part of my ancestry." Abby was genuinely confused.

"You can't tell anyone," her father insisted. "No one here knows. My whole life would be upended. No one will understand. You can't." He was really upset. "I'm not ready, Abby. This family is not ready."

Her dad stood up and hurried out the room. Abby heard his office door close.

"Mom, this really is not a big deal." Abby wanted to reassure her mom. "We have all kinds of kids at school. There's an entire LGBTQIA community in town. People are people. I mean, I *am* shocked. It's new to me. I have so many more questions. But you and dad don't have to keep it hidden."

Her mom took a deep breath. "Abby, you need to give this some time. Your dad has been very comfortable living life in the way we have."

"It's really not that healthy, Mom," Abby added. "You both need to be true to yourself. You need to be who you are. Are you always afraid someone will find out? That can't be a very happy way to live."

"Let me go talk to your dad. Are you sure you're all right with all this?"

Abby stood and hugged her mom. "Yes, Mom. I love you both."

# 12

Abby was in her room writing her essay on her family history. She heard a knock on her door.

"Come in."

Abby's parents entered.

"Can we talk some more?" her mom asked.

Abby shifted her chair back, so her parents could sit on her bed.

Her mom spoke first. "Your dad and I realize it's not up to us to decide how and when you share your family story. We want you to do what makes you comfortable. We just want you to really think about it. Once you share your story, it will be out there. You can't take it back. It will become a part of you."

Abby's dad got up, walked over to the window, and looked out.

Abby's mom continued. "Maybe things *have* changed. I hope they have anyway. Things like this weren't accepted not too long ago. You've probably figured out this is what caused an issue with Dad and his parents. They just couldn't understand us at all."

Abby's mom thought for a moment. "There will still be some people that won't approve of us. You may find some of your friends or their parents—or even some of your teachers—don't accept this. It could make life more complicated for you."

She looked Abby in the eyes. "That worries us the most. We worry for you. We don't want you to have problems because of us."

Abby shook her head. "This story is part of me. If someone has an issue with any of it—that's their problem. It's not mine. And it's not yours. It's their problem. You guys are great people. You do so much for everyone. I don't care what other people think. I think you'll be surprised to learn most people simply don't care."

"I hope so, Abby. Maybe times really have changed." Abby's mom took a deep breath. "We're willing to see what happens."

Abby's dad stood quietly. He was still looking out the window. After a few minutes, he turned around. "My mom really said to say hello to me?"

Abby smiled and nodded.

He smiled back. "I think I'll go call her."

# About The Author

Mary Francis lives on a quiet, dead-end road in Massachusetts surrounded by birdfeeders and windchimes. Besides writing, her other passions include hiking, wildlife photography, and family game nights (particularly when she wins!)

# My Dad's Secret

# About The Publisher

Story Shares is a nonprofit focused on supporting the millions of teens and adults who struggle with reading by creating a new shelf in the library specifically for them. The ever-growing collection features content that is compelling and culturally relevant for teens and adults, yet still readable at a range of lower reading levels.

Story Shares generates content by engaging deeply with writers, bringing together a community to create this new kind of book. With more intriguing and approachable stories to choose from, the teens and adults who have fallen behind are improving their skills and beginning to discover the joy of reading. For more information, visit storyshares.org.

Easy to Read. Hard to Put Down.

# My Dad's Secret

www.ingramcontent.com/pod-product-compliance
Lightning Source LLC
Chambersburg PA
CBHW071226170626
46809CB00005BA/1950